DATE DUE			
DEC 4 '85			
NOV 21 '86			
JAN 12 '87			
JAN 15 '87			
APR 28 '87			
MAY 14 '87			
OCT 29 '87			
JAN 11 '88			
FEB 16 '88			
MAY 12 '88			
Sokol			
JAN 1 4			
MAY 1 2			

E
HOG

Hoguet, Susan
Ramsay.

I unpacked my
grandmother's trunk.

482588 042808

Chapter II 1985-86

I Unpacked My Grandmother's Trunk

A PICTURE BOOK GAME

by Susan Ramsay Hoguet

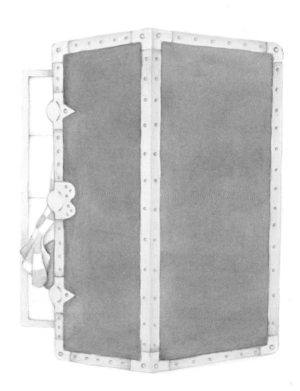

E. P. DUTTON, INC. • NEW YORK

for Ramsay and Alexander Livingston,
with thanks to Debbie

Library of Congress Cataloging in Publication Data
Hoguet, Susan Ramsay.
   I unpacked my grandmother's trunk.

   Summary: From grandmother's trunk are taken objects
beginning with each letter of the alphabet. Directions
for playing this game are included.
   [1. Trunks (Luggage)—Fiction.   2. Alphabet.
3. Games]   I. Title.
PZ7.H6847Iad   1983   [E]   83-1701
ISBN 0-525-44069-0

Published simultaneously in Canada by
Fitzhenry & Whiteside Limited, Toronto

Published simultaneously in Canada by Clarke,
Irwin & Company Limited, Toronto and Vancouver

Editor: Ann Durell   Designer: Claire Counihan

Printed by Dai Nippon Printing Co., Ltd., Tokyo, Japan.
First Edition
10 9 8 7 6 5 4 3 2 1

Directions for playing
I Unpacked My Grandmother's Trunk

This game can be played with two or more players. It is an excellent car game.

The first player says, "I unpacked my grandmother's trunk, and out of it I took an acrobat" (or any other object beginning with *a*).

The second player says, "I unpacked my grandmother's trunk, and out of it I took an acrobat and a bear" (or any other object beginning with *b*).

The third player (or the first, if only two are playing) says, "I unpacked my grandmother's trunk, and out of it I took an acrobat, a bear, and a cloud" (or any other object beginning with *c*).

Each player in turn adds a new object for the appropriate letter of the alphabet after listing *all* the previously named objects. The first time a player forgets to mention a previously named object or mentions one in the wrong order, that player must drop out of the game. The last player still in the game is the winner.

If using this book for the game, players should first go through the book, then close it and play the game from memory.

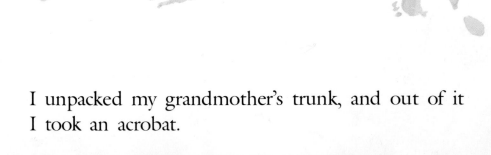

I unpacked my grandmother's trunk, and out of it
I took an acrobat.

an acrobat and a bear.

an acrobat, a bear, and a cloud.

an acrobat, a bear, a cloud, and a dinosaur.

an acrobat, a bear, a cloud, a dinosaur, and an eagle.

Goodings Grove School
Homer District 33C
Lockport, Illinois

an acrobat, a bear, a cloud, a dinosaur, an eagle,
and a fairy.

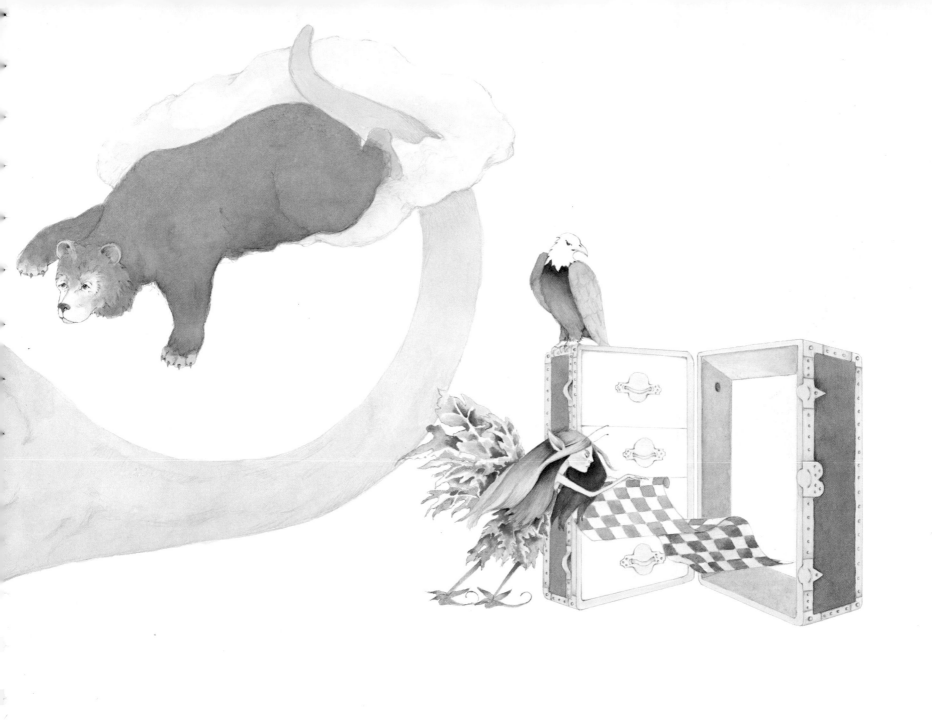

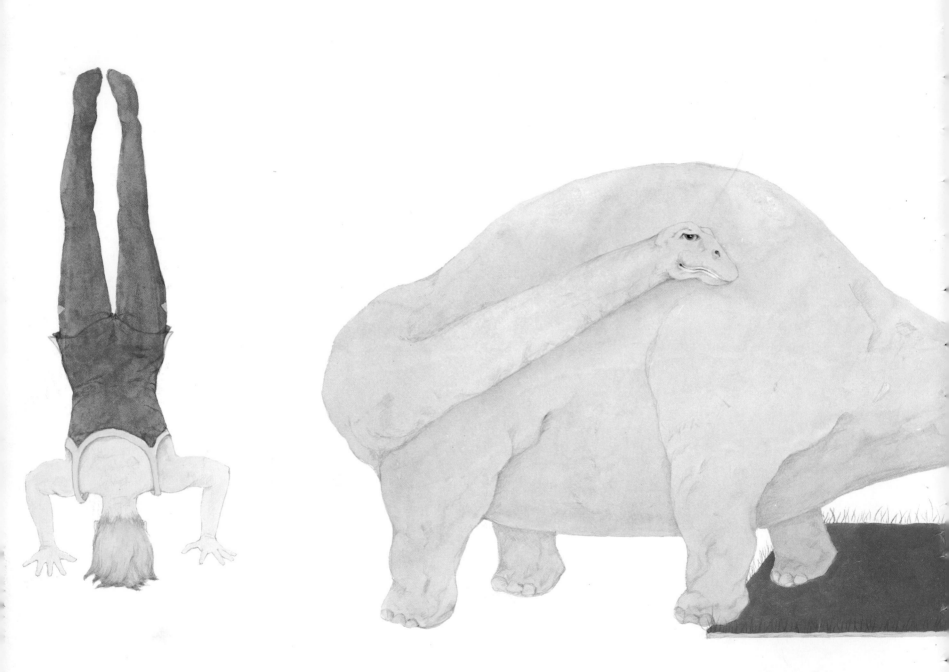

an acrobat, a bear, a cloud, a dinosaur, an eagle, a fairy, and some grass.

an acrobat, a bear, a cloud, a dinosaur, an eagle, a fairy, some grass, and a hat.

an acrobat, a bear, a cloud, a dinosaur, an eagle, a fairy, some grass, a hat, and an igloo.

an acrobat, a bear, a cloud, a dinosaur, an eagle, a fairy,
some grass, a hat, an igloo, and a jungle.

an acrobat, a bear, a cloud, a dinosaur, an eagle, a fairy, some grass, a hat, an igloo, a jungle, and a kangaroo.

an acrobat, a bear, a cloud, a dinosaur, an eagle, a fairy, some grass, a hat, an igloo, a jungle, a kangaroo, and a lamp.

an acrobat, a bear, a cloud, a dinosaur, an eagle, a fairy,
some grass, a hat, an igloo, a jungle, a kangaroo, a lamp,
and a mouse.

an acrobat, a bear, a cloud, a dinosaur, an eagle, a fairy, some grass, a hat, an igloo, a jungle, a kangaroo, a lamp, a mouse, and a nest.

an acrobat, a bear, a cloud, a dinosaur, an eagle, a fairy,
some grass, a hat, an igloo, a jungle, a kangaroo, a lamp,
a mouse, a nest, and an ostrich.

an acrobat, a bear, a cloud, a dinosaur, an eagle, a fairy, some grass, a hat, an igloo, a jungle, a kangaroo, a lamp, a mouse, a nest, an ostrich, and a pagoda.

an acrobat, a bear, a cloud, a dinosaur, an eagle, a fairy,
some grass, a hat, an igloo, a jungle, a kangaroo, a lamp,
a mouse, a nest, an ostrich, a pagoda, and a queen.

an acrobat, a bear, a cloud, a dinosaur, an eagle, a
fairy, some grass, a hat, an igloo, a jungle, a kangaroo,
a lamp, a mouse, a nest, an ostrich, a pagoda, a queen,

and a rocking chair.

an acrobat, a bear, a cloud, a dinosaur, an eagle, a
fairy, some grass, a hat, an igloo, a jungle, a kangaroo,
a lamp, a mouse, a nest, an ostrich, a pagoda, a queen,

a rocking chair, and a snowman.

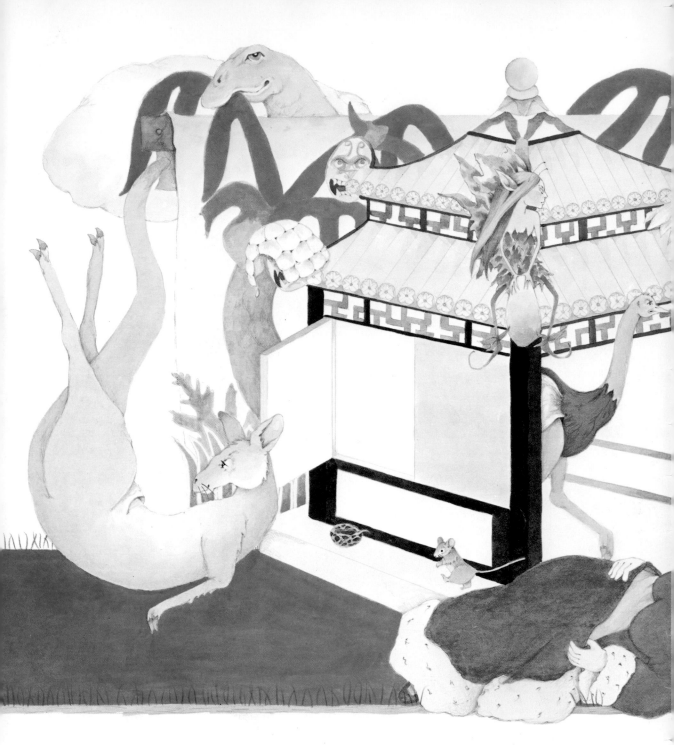

an acrobat, a bear, a cloud, a dinosaur, an eagle, a
fairy, some grass, a hat, an igloo, a jungle, a kangaroo,
a lamp, a mouse, a nest, an ostrich, a pagoda, a queen,

a rocking chair, a snowman, and a tiger.

an acrobat, a bear, a cloud, a dinosaur, an eagle, a
fairy, some grass, a hat, an igloo, a jungle, a kangaroo,
a lamp, a mouse, a nest, an ostrich, a pagoda, a queen,

a rocking chair, a snowman, a tiger, and an umbrella.

an acrobat, a bear, a cloud, a dinosaur, an eagle, a
fairy, some grass, a hat, an igloo, a jungle, a kangaroo,
a lamp, a mouse, a nest, an ostrich, a pagoda, a queen,

a rocking chair, a snowman, a tiger, an umbrella, and
a valentine.

an acrobat, a bear, a cloud, a dinosaur, an eagle, a
fairy, some grass, a hat, an igloo, a jungle, a kangaroo,
a lamp, a mouse, a nest, an ostrich, a pagoda, a queen,

a rocking chair, a snowman, a tiger, an umbrella, a
valentine, and a windmill.

an acrobat, a bear, a cloud, a dinosaur, an eagle, a fairy, some grass, a hat, an igloo, a jungle, a kangaroo, a lamp, a mouse, a nest, an ostrich, a pagoda, a queen,

a rocking chair, a snowman, a tiger, an umbrella, a
valentine, a windmill, and a xylophone.

an acrobat, a bear, a cloud, a dinosaur, an eagle, a
fairy, some grass, a hat, an igloo, a jungle, a kangaroo,
a lamp, a mouse, a nest, an ostrich, a pagoda, a queen,

a rocking chair, a snowman, a tiger, an umbrella, a valentine, a windmill, a xylophone, and a yo-yo.

an acrobat, a bear, a cloud, a dinosaur, an eagle, a
fairy, some grass, a hat, an igloo, a jungle, a kangaroo,
a lamp, a mouse, a nest, an ostrich, a pagoda, a queen,

a rocking chair, a snowman, a tiger, an umbrella, a valentine, a windmill, a xylophone, a yo-yo, and a zebra.

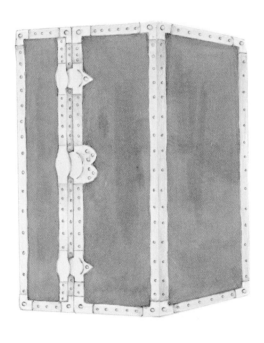